As they walk through a hush descends on them and their pace becomes slower. Salisbury Cathedral is a place of peace. One July morning, when the sun was very hot, a lorry stopped to deliver its goods to a little book shop by the gate. The driver was unaware that he had a very frightened passenger on board.

Cedric twitched his little nose and peered out from behind a box of books. He blinked his eyes in the bright sunlight. It had been a long journey from London and he had been so afraid that he might be squashed by some of the packets and boxes of books. He hadn't really intended to come to Salisbury. Because he was a very nosy mouse he had crept onto the lorry to look around and it seemed like a good place for a sleep.

Now he was a hungry mouse and his tummy gurgled and called for food. A little girl went past with an ice-cream and the cornet crumpled in her hand. Cedric watched hungrily as pieces of cornet fell into the gutter.

Cedric became very agitated. He needed to taste that food and yet he was very scared. Gradually he edged his way to the door and with a big leap jumped into the gutter. He pulled the food in through the bars of the drain. It was dark in there but not smelly. Cedric found a tiny ledge to sit on. The cornet was delicious. Soon he forgot that he'd come to a strange new place and left all his friends behind.

"Psst......PSST......!" He looked into the darkness.

"Who are you?" he asked, as he saw the outline of another mouse.

"I might ask you the same question," came the reply, "AND I do NOT like strangers taking my food."

Cedric was normally very placid but he was SO hungry, and he angrily retorted, "Your food! I was the one who saw it fall and pulled it in here. I've come a very long way . . . from LONDON! and my name is Cedric."

"From London," gasped the other mouse. "Why I've never seen a London mouse before. I'm sorry I was unfriendly. Let me introduce myself.

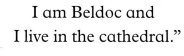

I am Beldoc and
I live in the cathedral."

Now it was Cedric's turn to be surprised. "THE CATHEDRAL!! Oh how wonderful. My cousin used to live in a cathedral called St Paul's, in London. We lived in St James' Park, where it is quieter and people leave food behind after their picnics."

Cedric was a kind mouse really and he pushed the cornet round the ledge to Beldoc. "Share this with me, it's very good."

They munched in silence and every now and again the drain became dark as a human stepped on the grating above them. When they could eat no more Beldoc said, "Are you going back to London?"

"I'd like to," replied Cedric, "but I'm a nosy mouse and I'd like to have a look around here first."

"Well let's wait until just before dark" suggested Beldoc, "and then you can meet my family and friends."

At dusk they climbed out of the drain and ran along the gutter, through the gate and into the cathedral grounds. It was very quiet but as they reached the grass Cedric froze. In front of them a large ginger cat was lying on the path.

Beldoc laughed, "Come on Cedric," he called over his shoulder, "this is Marmaduke, he's our friend. Everyone here calls him Marmie."

Cedric thought cathedral mice must be crazy but he ran as fast as he could after Beldoc. Suddenly a terrific noise sounded overhead. He jumped and flattened himself into the side of the pathway against the grass.

Beldoc came back. "You'll have to get used to the noise. It's only bell ringing practice. It will be worse on Sunday."

Cedric wasn't at all sure he would stay until Sunday!

At the cathedral door, Cedric was surprised to see tall mice, short mice, fat mice and thin mice, all smiling and holding out their hands. Beldoc proudly introduced his new companion.

The mice took him inside the cathedral and tiptoed along the corridor.

"We live here in the cloisters," said Beldoc. It was such a lovely place that Cedric squeezed himself to prove he wasn't dreaming.

They came to a paving slab with a small hole near its edge. The mice disappeared into the hole, followed by Cedric.

Underneath the slab the mice had a lovely home, which Bella liked to call Mouse Villa. The blankets on the beds of the baby mice were edged in a gold thread. Cedric fingered it and Beldoc whispered, "We found a piece of material by the altar and when we pulled a thread we found we had a lovely long gold thread which we stitched onto the blankets."

"It's lovely" said Cedric, and he sipped the dandelion milk that Beldoc's wife, Bella, had made for him. Soon he was fast asleep.

In the morning he awoke late and found Miss Sarah, the teacher mouse, teaching the mouse children a rhyme. She did this to teach the children the history of their lovely home.

"As many windows in this church we see,
As days within one year there be,
As many marble pillars here appear,
As hours throughout the fleeting year,
As many gates as moons one year does view,
Strange tale to tell, yet no more strange than true."

"Oh" whispered Cedric. "You are so clever!"

She smiled, "I found it on a postcard that a tourist dropped, and I checked and found that it's true!"

After lessons Miss Sarah showed Cedric and the children some interesting things. "You must not miss these things," she said, as only school teachers do. "This medieval clock," she told Cedric "is the oldest clock in England but it doesn't have a face. It tells us the hours and the mouse children learn to count. We have singing lessons too. Our class is beneath the organ. It's a bit noisy but no-one hears the mouse children when they sing. The little choir boys come in to sing quite often and now little girls come in too. Sometimes they see us but they do not shout or scream. If we are really lucky they drop a sweet that they have smuggled in. That's a real treat!"

Cedric was happy he'd come to Salisbury. What tales he'd be able to tell the mice in St James' Park. The day just whizzed by.

Soon Cedric and the other mice were tucked up in their beds and all was quiet.

THUD, THUD, a noise thundered over his head. Cedric rubbed his eyes and looked around. Everyone else was asleep. He crept out of his tiny fragrant bed, which was a pot-pourri box. Bella had told him they had found it in the nearby gift shop. At the entrance to Mouse Villa he watched a man shut the big wooden doors at the far end of the cloisters. It was very dark and very quiet. He ran down the flagstones and crept through a tiny hole. Inside the cathedral he felt very tiny. He'd never been in such a big house before.

After a while he found a way outside and bumped into Marmie who was very worried.

"It's the light you see," the old cat cried.

"What light?" enquired Cedric.

"Well it's THE light, the one on top of the spire. It shines every night to show everyone where the cathedral is and I think it stops aeroplanes from bumping into it. Well tonight it's out. I don't know what to do. What a responsibility! I just want a quiet life. I don't need this worry!"

Cedric thought hard for a moment.

"We have to tell someone . . . don't we?" he suggested.

"Of course, of course," said Marmie, "but how?"

"I will go and wake the others," Cedric answered, and he scampered away.

Back at Mouse Villa he woke the whole family.

"Quickly, we have to do something, a plane might hit your lovely cathedral, and people will not know where to come to say their prayers. THE LIGHT'S OUT," he squeaked and jumped up and down.

Beldoc scratched his head and thought.

Bella scratched her head and thought.

13

Miss Sarah the teacher mouse thought.

Even Uncle Tobias thought, but no-one had an answer.

Suddenly Cedric leapt up on to his bed and stretched out his hands.

"I've got the answer."

The mice looked at him wondering what it was.

"Well, in London where I come from," said Cedric, "there are many shops and if the mice get into them all the alarms go off. The noise is worse than your bells on Sunday! It makes people come to see what's the matter."

"But this is a cathedral, not a shop," said Uncle Tobias.

"Yes, but Bella said my sweet smelling bed came from the gift shop, right here in the cathedral."

It was only minutes later when they were all gathered around the gift shop door. There was no way in.

"We will have to eat our way in," said Uncle Tobias.

So they gnawed and gnawed until they made a small hole in the side of the door frame. They scampered inside.

The child mice went straight to the chocolate but Uncle Tobias looked at them severely.

They ran over the cash till and amongst the books.

Round and round, round and around, they went, it seemed for hours. The alarm started to ring.

Round and round they went again, holding hands in a big circle.

Suddenly the door opened and a crowd of policemen and other people rushed in.

They ran back down the corridor and into the cloisters and down
their hole.

They sat on their little beds and waited.

People were walking about over their heads.

"It's only mice," one man said, "there's no-one here. We'll have to
stop giving that cat so much food. He doesn't seem to catch the mice
any more."

The people talked a bit longer and then went out of the big wooden
door at the end of the corridor.

Cedric and Beldoc looked at each other.

"Well the people came but they didn't see the light was out. What
can we do now?"

"I thought it would work," cried Cedric.

Then the door opened again and the voices got closer.

"It's the first time that has happened," said one voice, "we will have to get it fixed immediately. The light always has to shine. Salisbury has the tallest cathedral spire and everyone knows that its red light glows and can be seen for miles and miles."

Cedric and Beldoc hugged each other.

"It worked, it worked. Now we can go back to bed until morning."

As they drank their dandelion milk for breakfast they were all smiling, except for Cedric.

"Why are you not happy?" said Beldoc.

"I think I must go back to London. Everyone will be wondering where I am," Cedric replied.

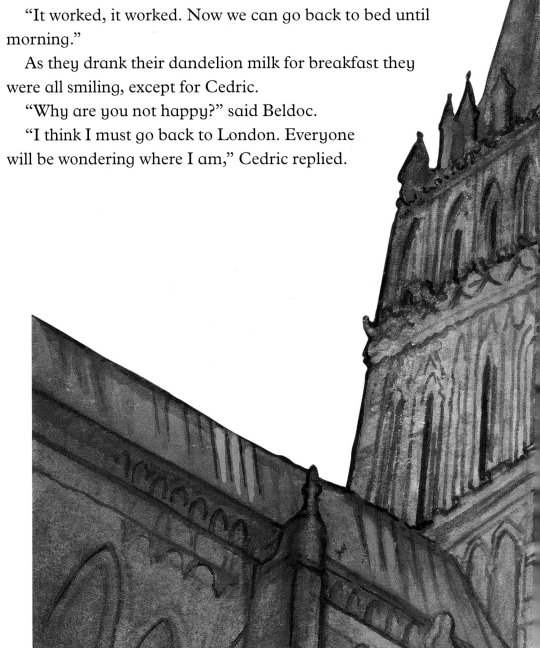

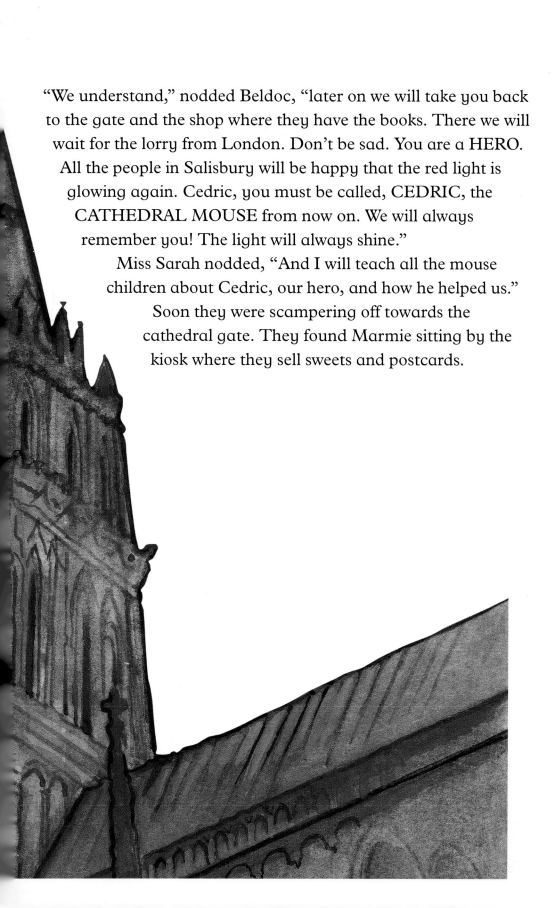

"We understand," nodded Beldoc, "later on we will take you back to the gate and the shop where they have the books. There we will wait for the lorry from London. Don't be sad. You are a HERO. All the people in Salisbury will be happy that the red light is glowing again. Cedric, you must be called, CEDRIC, the CATHEDRAL MOUSE from now on. We will always remember you! The light will always shine."

Miss Sarah nodded, "And I will teach all the mouse children about Cedric, our hero, and how he helped us."

Soon they were scampering off towards the cathedral gate. They found Marmie sitting by the kiosk where they sell sweets and postcards.

"I am going home," said Cedric, "I'm sorry to be leaving you."

"I'm not sorry," hissed Marmie.

The mice were all amazed.

"WHY, MARMIE, WHY?" they cried.

"Well I have not had my breakfast or my milk. They said that I have to catch mice and I am not doing my job."

The mice gasped.

"Oh dear, Marmie. We will save you some scraps from people's picnics. After all you are a hero too! Without you and Cedric the light would not have been mended and the spire would have been dark all night."

Marmie liked this attention and began to feel better.

"Might you save ALL the FISH sandwiches?"

"Of course," said Beldoc, "and we will keep out of sight and the humans will think you have caught us. Then they will give you milk again."